Published in 2022 by Groundwood Books /
House of Anansi Press
groundwoodbooks.com

Groundwood Books respectfully acknowledges that the land on
which we operate is the Traditional Territory of many Nations,
including the Anishinabeg, the Wendat and the Haudenosaunee.
It is also the Treaty Lands of the Mississaugas of the Credit.

We acknowledge for their financial support of our publishing
program the Canada Council for the Arts, the Ontario Arts
Council and the Government of Canada.

Canada Council **Conseil des Arts**
for the Arts **du Canada**

ONTARIO ARTS COUNCIL
CONSEIL DES ARTS DE L'ONTARIO
an Ontario government agency
un organisme du gouvernement de l'Ontario

With the participation of the Government of Canada
Avec la participation du gouvernement du Canada | **Canadä**

Library and Archives Canada Cataloguing in Publication
Title: Flock / story by Sara Cassidy ; pictures by Geraldo Valério.
Names: Cassidy, Sara, author. | Valério, Geraldo, illustrator.
Identifiers: Canadiana (print) 20210230452 | Canadiana (ebook)
20210230517 | ISBN 9781773064406 (hardcover) |
ISBN 9781773064413 (EPUB) | ISBN 9781773064420 (Kindle)
Classification: LCC PS8555.A7812 F56 2022 | DDC jC813/.6—dc23

The illustrations were created with acrylic paint, color pencil
and paper collage.
Design by Michael Solomon and Lucia Kim
Printed and bound in South Korea

MIX
Paper from
responsible sources
FSC FSC® C013572
www.fsc.org

For Joseph, Nicholas and
Sofia, with love — SC

Flock

"Yuck, crust!"

Story by **Sara Cassidy**

Pictures by **Geraldo Valério**

GROUNDWOOD BOOKS
HOUSE OF ANANSI PRESS
TORONTO / BERKELEY

"Hello! I'm Mika. You really like crusts. I'm going to name you Serious."

strut
peck
strut

peck peck

"Hi! I'll call you Fancy. Would you like some lettuce?"

bob

"Hello, Curious.
How about a
cracker?"

scratch

hoo

"Hey! Hoot! Shouldn't you be asleep?"

twee
twee

gobble

"Here, catch!
I name you Wild."

grunt

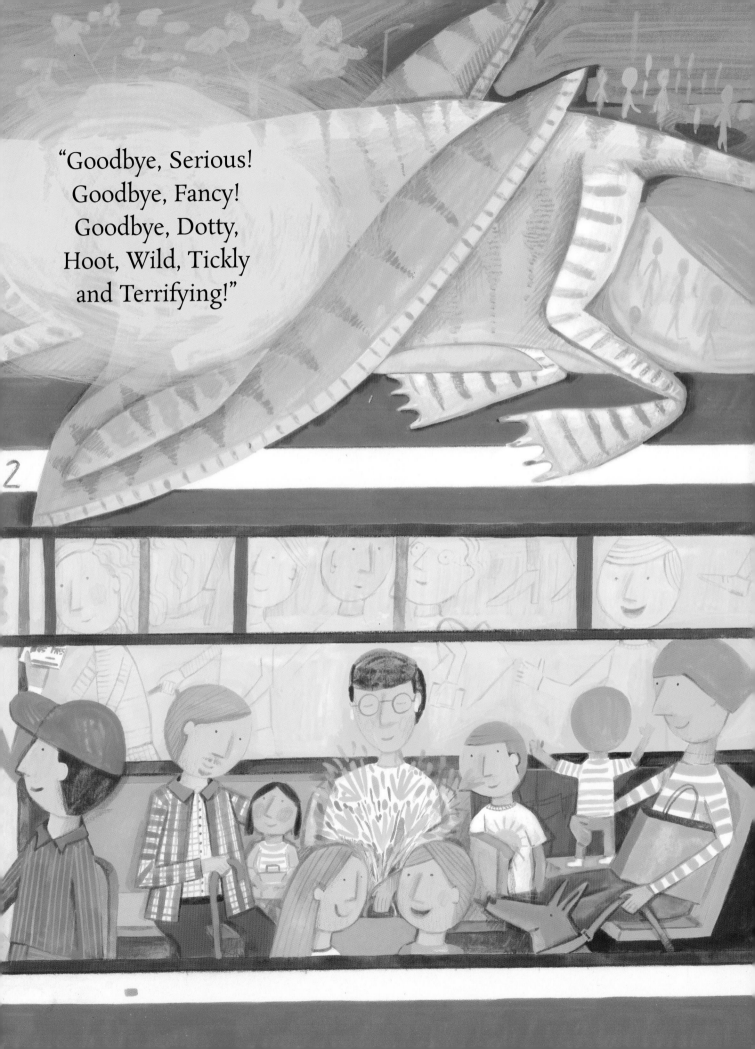

"Goodbye, Serious!
Goodbye, Fancy!
Goodbye, Dotty,
Hoot, Wild, Tickly
and Terrifying!"

"Mom, I'm hungry."

"What happened to your lunch?"